A Good & Perfect Gift

A Good & Perfect Gift

By Drew Bacigalupa   Illustrated by Jeannie Pear

Our Sunday Visitor, Inc.
Huntington, Indiana 46750

© Copyright Our Sunday Visitor, Inc. 1978

ISBN: 0-87973-352-7
Library of Congress Catalog Card Number: 78-60727

Illustrations by Jeannie Pear

Published, printed and bound in the U.S.A. by
Our Sunday Visitor, Inc.
Noll Plaza
Huntington, Indiana 46750

352

For our daughters,
and for their daughters

SHE was a little bit mad
at *Santo Niño*. It was Christmas
morning and she'd already opened
the one gift under their tree
at home. That didn't seem
like much — a winter sweater
which she needed anyway,
no toy, and no sign of the Daddy
she'd asked for. She could
excuse Santa Claus, maybe he just
forgot, but *El Santo Niño*
wasn't supposed to forget anything.

And it seemed she'd been asking
for him as long as she could
remember — not for something
impossible, like Mama said,
not for a Daddy she could have
all the time like the other kids,
just for a Daddy for one day,
for Christmas day.

It was cold in church
and the Mass was long,
and Mama kept her head bowed,
crying. If she fidgeted,
Mama reproved her sharply,
"Manuelita!", and made her
look again at the *Nacimiento.*

But Manuelita wasn't happy about
that Baby. He had both father
and mother, and lots of *pastores*
keeping them company, and sheep
and a cow and a *burro*,
and shiny lighted stars over
his stable, and a tree behind that
was bigger and prettier than hers.

And when she looked away, she saw
other little girls in church
standing next to daddies,
or being held by them,
and carrying in their arms
the most beautiful dolls
in the whole wide world.

14

After Mass, she and Mama
trudged through deep snow up the hill
to their *adobe* at the edge
of the village. *Piñon* smoke was
coming from every chimney but theirs.
Mama held her hand tightly,
but they were silent. Manuelita
didn't want silence on Christmas
and wondered if the radio batteries
were still working. Mama had
kept it on a long time last night.
She was thinking of that and of how
maybe she could hear some carols
or stories when Mama pushed open
their door, and gasped in fright!

Peering around her frayed *rebozo*,
Manuelita saw a man standing
at their kitchen table, facing them
with a gun in his hand.
Santo Niño had remembered.
It was her Christmas Daddy.

HE was very tall, almost as high
as the roof *vigas*, and had a
big black mustache and heavy, dark
eyebrows. He carried a bag, too—
not stuffed with toys
like Santa Claus', but with other things,
maybe presents. Manuelita could
see a blanket roll, a hatchet,
some tins of food and the bloodied pelt
of a rabbit he'd probably killed
recently with that gun.

He and Mama were talking fast,
saying funny things like,
"It's on the radio; I know who you are,"
and "If you'll let me stay a little
while, I won't hurt anyone."
Mama thought he was a bad man,
and didn't like him, and
Manuelita, wanting to explain
who he really was, kept trying
to get her attention by pulling
at her arm. After a while
they stopped talking and stared
at each other. Then Mama just sat
in a chair, like she was very tired
and couldn't move.

Manuelita went to her side and
whispered in her ear that he was
her Christmas present, the Daddy
she'd asked *Santo Niño* to give her
for just this one day.
Mama cried again, but she didn't speak.
Then she wiped her eyes with
the back of her hand and crossed
the room to a pot of *frijoles*
she'd been preparing before Mass.
The man hitched the gun in his belt
and pulled the rabbit from the bag
and spilled out all the
canned foods on the kitchen table.

Mama wouldn't let her go with him,
but Manuelita watched from the
frosted window when he ran to the
woods behind their house
and came back with armloads of *piñon*.
He set the logs ablaze in their
corner fireplace and stood with his
back to it, keeping warm.
Manuelita went and stood beside him,
putting her hands behind her
as he did, spreading her feet
in the widest possible stance.

MAMA glanced at her and started
to speak, but then was silent
and turned again to preparing
the meal. For the first time,
though she'd never stopped looking
at him, the man's eyes rested on
Manuelita. "We have a little
Christmas tree, but no *Nacimiento*,"
she said. "That's not right, is it?"
"No, *mi hija*," the big man
answered, "but perhaps we can
do something about that."

Maybe her Daddy was a *santero*,

the kind Mama had told

her about, who carved saints

from the soft cottonwood and took them

off the mountain down into the city

where *gringos* and places

called museums paid good money for them.

He must be one because nobody else

could put a knife to plain old wood

and so soon have it looking

like real people, better

than the *santos* in the village church!

She watched his big hands shaping
the delicate contours of the Baby,
marveling that *Santo Niño* had sent
her a Daddy better than all
the others in the village,
where they had no *santero*.
And when she picked up shavings,
the man took her frail hands
into his rough, calloused ones
and showed her how to fashion
simple ornaments from scraps of wood
tied together with thread.
All afternoon they huddled
by the fireplace, busy at work.

Manuelita made enough ornaments
to decorate the small tree
from top to bottom all around,
and when they stirred,
the raw wood picked up glints
of firelight, like little stars
dancing among the green boughs.
The man completed a *Niño*,
a beautiful Babe on a bed of straw,
and began to carve *Nuestra Señora*.
He smoked a big, brown pipe as he
worked, and let the child hold flaming
kindling to relight it each time
he packed it with fresh tobacco.

At one moment during
the darkening day, Manuelita heard
a rare and lovely sound in the room.
When she looked up,
it was Mama singing softly
to herself as she patted out
tortillas at the kitchen table.

They had a grand *comida*;
the rabbit was very good, tender,
with lots of it in every *taco*.
Mama had added some of
Daddy's dried *chili* to the *frijoles*,
and Manuelita savored the
pungent flavor in her mouth.
No one spoke much,
which did not seem unusual
to Manuelita, but occasionally
the man made a silly joke
and they all laughed.

MANUELITA knew that this

was the best meal of her life,

and the best day she'd ever lived.

One tiny disappointment

clouded her joy,

but she could not bring herself

to speak of it.

Night was coming, Christmas was ending,

and there wouldn't be time

for Daddy to finish the *Nacimiento*.

There'd be only *Maria*

and *Jesuscristo*,

mother and child like Mama and herself,

without a *San José*, without a father.

She wanted to stay awake
through the last minute of the evening,
but fatigue claimed her
and she lay down sleepily
before the fire. Mama covered her
with an old *poncho*. Manuelita watched
her mother and the man sit opposite
each other at the table,
not speaking, but listening to carols
on the radio. Sometimes, when there
were news broadcasts, they
turned the volume up and exchanged
solemn glances. Manuelita
fell asleep with the vision
of firelight radiantly bathing Mama
and her beautiful, strong Daddy.

The fire was almost out

when she woke,

the room dimly lighted,

and the man was gone.

She was on her cot;

he must have carried her there,

for scraps of his pipe tobacco

were on her blanket.

She scooped them up as treasures.

Mama slept soundly

on her narrow bed across the room.

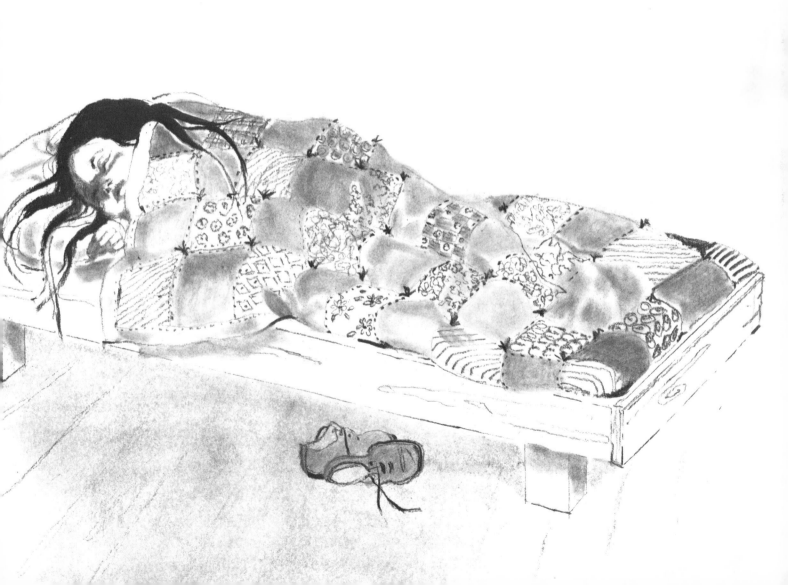

Manuelita felt no sorrow
that the man was gone,
only joy that she'd had a Daddy
on Christmas day.
She got up and tiptoed
across the room to see again
the *Nacimiento* and thank *El Santo Niño*
for answering her prayers.

And there with *Nuestra Señora*
and the Infant was a third carving,
unfinished, only roughly blocked out,
with no facial features and no details.
But it was unmistakably *San José*,
the father of the family, standing tall beside *Maria*,
his head bowed toward *El Niño*.
Mama had lighted a vigil candle
before them, and for a long time
Manuelita sat and stared
at the beautiful figures.

Spanish words in order of their appearance in the story:

Word	How to pronounce it	What it means
El Santo Niño	el san-toh neen-yoh	the Holy Child
Nacimiento	nah-cee-mien-toh	birth; here referring to the Christmas creche or nativity "crib."
pastores	pass-tor-aes	shepherds
burro	boo-row	donkey
adobe	ah-dough-bee	mud house commonly built in New Mexico, made of mud and straw which are shaped into bricks
piñon	peen-yon	an evergreen tree common to New Mexico
rebozo	reh-boh-soh	a shawl worn by girls and women in both New Mexico and Mexico
vigas	vee-gahs	natural wood beams in the ceiling
frijoles	free-hole-ess	beans
mi hija	me ee-hah	my daughter
santero	sahn-tear-row	wood carver who makes saints; an old craft in New Mexico
gringos	green-gos	slang: North Americans, Anglos

santos	sahn-tos	saints; here referring to wood carvings of saints
Niño	neen-yoh	Child, here referring to child Jesus,
Nuestra Señora	noo-ess-tra sen-yora	Our Lady, the mother of Jesus
tortillas	tor-tee-yas	pancake-like dough, which is eaten rather than bread; often it is wrapped around beans
comida	ko-mee-dah	meal
taco	taa-koh	a *tortilla* wrapped around meat and beans
chili	chee-lee	hot peppers
Maria	mah-ree-iah	Mary
Jesucristo	heh-zoo-krees-toh	Jesus Christ
San José	san hoh-zeh	Saint Joseph
poncho	pon-cho	a sleeveless jacket with an opening for the head; worn in Mexico and New Mexico